Coat of
Many Colors

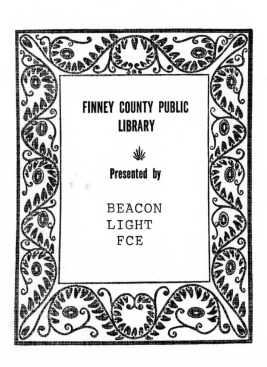

To my mother, Avie Lee Parton; to all the good mothers everywhere;
and to anyone who has suffered the emotional pain of being made fun of,
may this book be healing.

—*Dolly Parton*

For my mother, who sewed for me.

—*Judith P. Sutton*

Special thanks to Joanna Cotler, Kate Morgan Jackson, Heather Henson, and Harriett Barton.
Editor, Byron Preiss Visual Publications: Wendy Wax
Book Design: Judith Sutton
Art Director: Dean Motter

Library of Congress Cataloging-in-Publication Data
Parton, Dolly.
    Coat of many colors / by Dolly Parton ; illustrated by Judith Sutton.
        p.   cm.
    Summary: A poor girl delights in her coat of many colors, made by her
mother from rags, because despite the ridicule of the other children she
knows the coat was made with love.
    ISBN 0-06-023413-X. — ISBN 0-06-023414-8 (lib. bdg.)
    [1. Clothing and dress—Fiction.   2. Poor—Fiction.   3. Mothers and
daughters—Fiction.   4. Stories in rhyme.]   I. Sutton, Judith, date, ill.
II. Title.
PZ8.3.P2714Co   1994   93-3866
[E]—dc20   CIP
                                                                                          AC

1   2   3   4   5   6   7   8   9   10
First Edition

Dolly Parton

Coat of Many Colors

Illustrated by Judith Sutton

A Byron Preiss Book

HarperCollinsPublishers

Back through the years
I go wandering once again,
back to the season of my youth.

I recall a box of rags
that someone gave us,
and how my mama
put the rags to use.

There were rags of many colors,
but every piece was small,
and I didn't have a coat
and it was way down in the fall.

Mama sewed the rags together,
she sewed every stitch with love,
and made my coat of many colors
that I was so proud of.

My coat of many colors
that my mama made for me,
made only from rags.
But I wore it so proudly.

And though we had no money,
I was rich as I could be,
in my coat of many colors
my mama made for me.

As she sewed she told a story
from the Bible she had read,
about a coat of many colors
Joseph wore, and then she said,

"Perhaps this coat will bring
you good luck and happiness."
And I couldn't wait to wear it
as she blessed it with a kiss.

So with patches on my britches
and holes in both my shoes,
and my coat of many colors
I hurried off to school,

just to find the children laughing
and making fun of me
in my coat of many colors
that my mama made for me.

And I didn't understand it
for I felt that I was rich.
And I told them of the love
that mama sewed in every stitch.

And I told them all the story
mama told me as she sewed.
And how my coat of many colors
was worth more than all their gold.

But they didn't understand it
and I tried to make them see
that one is only poor
if they choose to be.

And though we had no money
I was rich as I could be
in my coat of many colors
that mama made for me.

Through life I've remained happy
and good luck is on my side.
I have everything that anyone
could ever want from life.

But nothing is as precious
as my mama's memory,
and my coat of many colors
that mama made for me.